Frosty Whispers

Frosty Whispers

Matthew Petchinsky

Frosty Whispers: A Winter's Tale
By: Matthew Petchinsky

Introduction: The Murmurs of Winter

Winter is a season of contrasts—a time of silence and song, stillness and movement, harsh cold and comforting warmth. It blankets the world in white, painting a serene canvas upon which stories unfold, whispered by the wind. These whispers, delicate as frost-laden spider-webs and yet powerful enough to stir the soul, carry more than just the howling of the northern gales or the gentle sighs of snow-laden boughs. They carry secrets. Wishes. Warnings.

For centuries, humanity has spun tales about these frosty murmurs. Some say they are the voices of ancestors, guiding the living through the dark months. Others insist they are the echoes of the earth itself, mourning the fall of the sun and yearning for its return. But the truth lies deeper, hidden within the heart of winter's icy embrace—a truth shrouded in mystery and guarded by a realm unseen by most.

The whispers of winter are not mere folklore. They are the breath of a magical world that stirs to life only in the season of frost. This hidden domain, veiled by drifting snow and shimmering auroras, is where the essence of winter is born. It is a place of crystalline forests and glacial rivers, of twinkling stars that seem close enough to touch and moon-lit skies alive with spectral dances of light. It is the realm of the Frost-bound, an ancient race of beings whose connection to the world is woven through the fabric of winter itself.

Few have ever glimpsed this realm, and fewer still have returned to tell its tale. Those who do speak of a power both awe-inspiring and ter-rifying—a power that shapes not only the icy landscapes of winter but also the hearts of those who dare to venture close. For within the Frost-bound's domain, the whispers on the wind are alive, carrying the voices of a magic older than time. They carry the weight of hopes and dreams, of warnings unheeded and promises kept. They beckon to the brave and the curious, drawing them into a journey that will test their courage, ignite their imagination, and forever change the way they see the world.

This is not just a story of winter but a story of discovery—of a young soul who hears these whispers not as faint echoes but as a clarion call to adventure. The journey begins with a question as fragile as the first snowflake of the season: What do the whispers of winter truly say?

In the pages that follow, we will unravel the mysteries of the icy winds, walk the snow-laden paths of courage and curiosity, and delve into the magic that lies dormant beneath the surface of frost and shadow. As you turn each page, let the murmurs of winter guide you, for they may hold more than just a story—they may hold the key to the enduring power of hope, the strength to embrace the unknown, and the courage to seek light even in the coldest of seasons.

Prepare yourself to step into winter's embrace, to hear its whispers, and to uncover the truth hidden within its frosted veil. The journey awaits, and the winds are calling.

Chapter 1: The Winter Wind's Warning

The town of Snowhaven sat nestled in a quiet valley, cradled by the ancient arms of snowcapped mountains. It was a place where winter always came early, frosting the rooftops and silencing the fields before autumn had a chance to say goodbye. But this year, winter's arrival was unusual—an early frost crept in overnight, its icy fingers touching even the most sheltered nooks of the quaint village. By morning, the air was sharp with cold, and the streets shimmered under a glaze of frost that sparkled like crushed diamonds in the pale sunlight.

Among the townsfolk who marveled at the early chill was Ellie Norwood, a bright-eyed girl with a heart as warm as her favorite woolen scarf. Ellie had always been attuned to the seasons, delighting in the rustle of fallen leaves or the patter of spring rain. But there was something about this frost that felt different, as if the air itself were alive with a strange energy.

Bundled in her thickest coat and mittens, Ellie stepped outside that morning and tilted her head toward the breeze. The wind, carrying the faintest scent of pine and something colder, almost metallic, seemed to hum in her ears. Then, just as she turned to head toward her grandfather's house, she heard it—a whisper, soft as the rustling of leaves yet clear as a bell.

"Beware the storm... eternal winter comes..."

Ellie froze. The voice wasn't one she recognized, yet it felt oddly familiar, like a long-forgotten melody. She spun around, but the street was empty save for a few early risers scraping frost from their windows. The wind whipped past her again, carrying another whisper.

"Danger... snow that never melts... the light must not fade..."

Her heart raced. Ellie had always been curious and imaginative, but this felt different from the make-believe worlds she often crafted in her mind. This felt real.

She hurried to her grandfather's house, a cozy cottage at the edge of town. The faint smell of cedar smoke greeted her as she pushed open the door, where she found Grandpa Arthur seated by the fireplace with a steaming mug of tea. A retired weatherman, Arthur was a fixture of Snowhaven, known for his precise forecasts and love of winter folklore.

"Ellie! What's got you rushing about on such a cold morning?" he asked, setting down his mug and beckoning her closer.

Ellie hesitated. She had shared her imaginings with others before, only to be met with indulgent smiles or gentle teasing. But her grandfather was different—he always listened.

"Grandpa," she began, sitting on the hearthrug, "have you ever heard whispers on the wind?"

Arthur's brows knitted together. "Whispers, you say? What kind of whispers?"

Ellie recounted what she had heard, her words tumbling out in a rush. As she spoke of warnings and eternal winter, she watched her grandfather's face shift from curiosity to something graver.

"When did you hear this?" he asked, his voice unusually serious.

"This morning, just before I came here," Ellie replied. "It sounded so real, Grandpa. Not like I imagined it—like someone was actually speaking to me through the wind."

Arthur rose from his chair and moved to the bookshelf, pulling out an old, leather-bound volume. Its spine was cracked with age, and the cover bore the faded image of a snowflake.

"You may not be imagining things, Ellie," he said, leafing through the pages. "There's an old legend about whispers carried by the winter wind. They say these murmurs come from a realm beyond our own, a place where winter's power is born. And sometimes, those whispers are warnings."

"A warning about what?" Ellie asked, her voice small.

Arthur paused, his finger tracing a passage in the book. "A storm," he said at last. "Not an ordinary blizzard, but a storm of magic. It's said that if this storm reaches its full fury, it can freeze entire towns in eternal winter, cutting them off from the sun forever."

Ellie's breath caught. "You think that's what I heard? A warning about this storm?"

Arthur nodded slowly. "It's possible. The early frost, the whispers... it all lines up. If the legends are true, then we must take this seriously."

But not everyone in Snowhaven was as willing to believe. When Ellie tried to share the whispers with her friends and neighbors, they laughed it off as another one of her fanciful stories. Only Grandpa Arthur stood by her, his belief rooted in years of studying weather patterns and folklore.

"Don't let their doubts shake you," he told her one evening as they watched the snow fall through the frosted window. "If the wind is speaking to you, Ellie, it's because it believes you can help. The question is, are you ready to listen?"

Ellie wasn't sure what listening would entail, but deep in her heart, she felt the stirrings of courage. The whispers had chosen her for a reason. And as the frost deepened and the wind grew colder, she resolved to uncover the truth behind the warnings.

Little did she know, this was only the beginning. The whispers of winter were not just warnings—they were a call to action, a prelude to an adventure that would test her bravery, unravel the secrets of Snowhaven, and reveal the hidden magic that lay within the icy heart of winter.

Chapter 2: The Whispering Woods

The Whispering Woods loomed at the edge of Snowhaven, a sprawling forest of towering evergreens that seemed darker and deeper than any forest Ellie had ever known. By day, its snow-laden branches glistened with an otherworldly beauty, but by night, the trees seemed to whisper secrets to the wind, their shadows stretching like the long fingers of some unseen presence. It was a place steeped in lore, a forest her grandfather often spoke of in his stories—stories of magic, danger, and the promise of answers hidden beneath the icy canopy.

Ellie had never dared venture into the woods alone. Few in Snowhaven did. But the whispers she had heard and the urgency in her grandfather's voice left her no choice. If the Frost Reaver and its coming storm were real, and if there truly was a way to stop it, she had to find it. Armed with a heavy coat, a flashlight, and her grandfather's old compass, Ellie set out at first light, her breath puffing in the frigid morning air.

The forest greeted her with an eerie stillness. The crunch of her boots on the snow felt deafening, and the wind seemed to grow softer, as though watching her every move. For a while, Ellie saw nothing unusual—just the towering pines and the faint sparkle of frost clinging to the branches. But as she ventured deeper, the atmosphere shifted. The air grew colder, sharper, almost biting. The trees stood taller, their trunks impossibly straight, and a faint blue light shimmered in the distance, like a pale aurora threading through the forest.

It was then that Ellie heard the whispers again.

This time, they were clearer, more insistent. The words danced on the edge of comprehension, like fragments of a forgotten song.

"Seek the Heart... restore the balance... beware the Reaver..."

Ellie clutched her flashlight tighter, her heart racing. She followed the whispers, letting them guide her steps deeper into the woods until she came to a small clearing. There, in the center of the glade, stood a peculiar figure no taller than her knee—a creature that seemed made entirely of snow and frost, its eyes glowing with a mischievous light.

"Ah, finally!" the creature exclaimed, its voice high-pitched but warm. "I was beginning to think you'd never arrive!"

Ellie blinked in surprise. "Who... what are you?"

The creature puffed out its chest proudly. "The name's Frostwick, snow sprite extraordinaire, keeper of frosty mischief, and occasional guide to curious humans. And you, my dear, are Ellie Norwood, granddaughter of Arthur the Weather-Wise. Yes, yes, I know all about you."

Ellie's mouth opened, then closed, then opened again. "How do you know my name?"

Frostwick grinned, revealing teeth that looked like tiny shards of ice. "The whispers told me, of course. You're the chosen one, aren't you? The one who's supposed to save Snowhaven from the Frost Reaver. Quite the honor, really."

Ellie frowned. "I don't even know what the Frost Reaver is, let alone how to stop it. I was hoping to find answers here."

"Well, aren't you in luck?" Frostwick said, twirling in place and sprinkling the air with snowflakes. "You've come to the right place. The Whispering Woods are ancient, you see, older than your little town, older than most things. This forest holds the key to winter's magic—and its balance. But that balance has been disrupted."

"By the Frost Reaver?" Ellie guessed.

"Exactly!" Frostwick said, nodding vigorously. "The Frost Reaver is a nasty spirit of ice and cold, born from the darkest corners of winter. It feeds on despair and darkness, growing stronger with every storm. If left unchecked, it will freeze Snowhaven—and the rest of the world—in eternal winter. No more spring, no more summer. Just endless cold."

Ellie shivered, not from the cold but from the weight of Frostwick's words. "How do we stop it?"

"That," Frostwick said, his tone growing serious, "is where the Heart of Winter comes in. The Heart is a magical artifact, the very essence of winter's power. It's what keeps the season in balance. If we can find it and restore its light, we can weaken the Frost Reaver and send it back to the shadows where it belongs."

"Where is the Heart of Winter?" Ellie asked.

"Ah, that's the tricky part," Frostwick said, scratching his icy head. "The Heart is hidden somewhere deep in the forest, protected by ancient wards and riddles. Only someone pure of heart and brave enough to face the dangers of the Whispering Woods can find it. Lucky for us, that's you."

Ellie swallowed hard. "Me? But I'm just a girl from Snowhaven. How am I supposed to do all that?"

Frostwick stepped closer, his glowing eyes meeting hers. "Because you've already started, Ellie. You heard the whispers when no one else did. You ventured into these woods when others wouldn't dare. And, most importantly, you care—not just about saving yourself, but about saving your town, your family, and even me, a scrappy little snow sprite."

Ellie felt a warmth in her chest, despite the cold. "Okay," she said, her voice steady. "I'll do it. I'll find the Heart of Winter and stop the Frost Reaver. But I'll need your help."

Frostwick grinned. "You can count on me, kiddo. Now, let's get moving. The forest doesn't like to wait, and neither does the Frost Reaver."

Together, they set off into the shimmering depths of the Whispering Woods, guided by whispers and the faint glow of Frostwick's magic. The journey ahead was fraught with uncertainty and danger, but Ellie felt a newfound sense of purpose. For the first time, she understood that the whispers of winter weren't just warnings—they were a call to action, a challenge to rise above fear and uncover the magic that lay within her own heart.

Chapter 3: The Frozen Labyrinth

The air grew colder as Ellie and Frostwick ventured deeper into the Whispering Woods, the trees giving way to an open expanse of glittering ice. Before them lay the Frozen Labyrinth, a sprawling maze of towering, crystalline walls that shimmered with a cold, pale light. Each icy surface reflected not only the forest around them but also strange, flickering images—ghostly visions that seemed to shift and change with every step.

"The Heart of Winter is hidden at the center of this labyrinth," Frostwick explained, his usually playful tone subdued. "But it's not just any maze. The Frozen Labyrinth is alive. It's meant to test you, Ellie. To see if you're worthy of wielding winter's power."

Ellie gazed at the maze, her breath fogging in the icy air. "What kind of tests?"

Frostwick sighed, his frosty form shimmering faintly. "Oh, you know, the usual—illusions to confuse you, puzzles to stump you, traps to make you doubt your every step. And if that's not enough, the labyrinth has a way of playing tricks on your mind, showing you your fears, your doubts. It's not exactly a winter wonderland, if you catch my drift."

Despite the sprite's attempt at humor, Ellie felt the weight of his words. This would be no simple journey. Still, she squared her shoulders, gripping the compass in her mittened hand. "Let's do this."

Entering the Labyrinth

As they stepped into the maze, the temperature dropped sharply, and the world around them seemed to hold its breath. The walls of ice were so tall they blocked out the sky, casting the labyrinth in an eerie, bluish glow. Every surface reflected distorted images of Ellie and Frostwick, their movements mirrored in strange, disjointed ways that made Ellie feel like she was being watched.

The first path split into three. Ellie instinctively moved toward the middle one, but Frostwick stopped her with a sharp tug on her coat.

"Not so fast," he said. "The labyrinth doesn't play fair. Sometimes the most obvious path leads to a dead end—or worse."

Ellie hesitated, closing her eyes to listen. For a moment, there was only silence. Then, faintly, the whispers returned.

"Left... take the left path..."

She opened her eyes, her heart pounding. "The whispers are guiding me," she said softly.

Frostwick nodded approvingly. "Good. Trust them. They're the voices of winter spirits, guardians of the labyrinth. If they're helping you, it means they believe in you."

Following the whispers, Ellie and Frostwick turned left, the passage narrowing as they moved deeper into the maze.

Illusions of Ice

The first challenge came in the form of a shimmering wall that appeared to block their path. The surface rippled like water, reflecting an image of Ellie standing alone, her breath fogging the air. Frostwick nudged her.

"It's an illusion," he said. "But you'll need to figure out how to break it."

Ellie stared at the wall, her reflection staring back. "How do I know it's not real?"

The whispers grew louder, urging her forward. She reached out tentatively, her hand passing through the icy surface as though it were made of mist. With a deep breath, Ellie stepped through the illusion, Frostwick following close behind.

On the other side, the whispers seemed to hum with approval.

"Not bad," Frostwick said, grinning. "But don't get too comfortable. The labyrinth has more tricks up its sleeve."

The Puzzle Gate

The next challenge was a gate made of interlocking ice crystals, each piece shimmering with faint symbols. A riddle was etched into the arch above:

To pass through, you must align the frost,
But choose poorly, and all is lost.

Ellie examined the gate, noting that the symbols resembled snowflakes, each one unique.

"Okay," she muttered, "align the frost... what does that mean?"

Frostwick floated closer, inspecting the gate. "I think it's a puzzle. You have to figure out which pieces go where. But be careful—one wrong move, and the gate will freeze shut."

Ellie closed her eyes again, listening for the whispers. This time, they seemed to guide her hands, urging her to move certain pieces into place. Slowly, methodically, she shifted the crystals, aligning them into a perfect snowflake pattern.

With a soft chime, the gate opened, the ice dissolving into mist.

"You're getting the hang of this," Frostwick said, his tone filled with pride.

The Traps of Doubt

As they ventured deeper, the labyrinth began to play on Ellie's emotions. One passage filled with a dense, swirling mist that whispered fears into her ears.

"You're not strong enough," the voices said. "You'll never find the Heart. Turn back while you can."

Ellie faltered, her courage wavering. But Frostwick's voice cut through the fog.

"Don't listen to them! The labyrinth is testing you. It wants to know if you'll give up."

Drawing a deep breath, Ellie focused on the whispers of the winter spirits instead. Their words were softer but clearer, a steady reassurance that guided her steps through the mist.

"You are brave. You are chosen. Keep going."

Finally, the mist cleared, revealing a spiral staircase of ice that led downward into the heart of the labyrinth.

The Heart of Winter

At the bottom of the staircase, Ellie and Frostwick entered a vast chamber bathed in a radiant, silvery-blue light. In the center of the room, suspended above a pedestal of ice, was the Heart of Winter—a crystalline orb that pulsed with an ethereal glow.

Ellie approached cautiously, feeling the whispers grow stronger, almost like a song. She reached out, her fingers grazing the surface of the orb. In that moment, a surge of warmth and power flooded through her, and the whispers crystallized into a single, clear voice.

"You have done well, Ellie," the voice said. "But your journey is not over. The Frost Reaver will come for this Heart. You must protect it, for it is the key to restoring balance."

As Ellie lifted the Heart of Winter from its pedestal, the chamber began to tremble. The walls of the labyrinth seemed to groan, and Frostwick's eyes widened in alarm.

"We need to get out of here," he said. "Now!"

Clutching the Heart tightly, Ellie followed Frostwick back up the staircase, the labyrinth shifting and collapsing around them. Each step was harder than the last, but Ellie refused to give up. She had come too far to fail now.

As they emerged from the labyrinth into the open forest, the whispers swirled around her, their tones both urgent and triumphant. Ellie knew the hardest part of her journey was yet to come, but for now, she held the Heart of Winter—and with it, the hope of saving Snowhaven.

Chapter 4: The Frost Reaver's Wrath

The chamber at the heart of the Frozen Labyrinth pulsed with an otherworldly energy. The crystalline walls shimmered as if alive, and the Heart of Winter floated just above its icy pedestal, glowing with an iridescent light that seemed to fill the entire space with warmth despite the bitter cold. Ellie stood in awe, the whispers of the winter spirits swirling around her in a melody that felt ancient and powerful. She reached out, feeling the pull of the artifact.

But just as her fingers brushed the surface of the Heart, the air around her froze—literally. Frost shot across the ground, snaking up the walls, and a bone-chilling cold sucked the warmth from the chamber. A deep, guttural voice echoed through the space, its tone laced with malice.

"So, the little human has come to play hero," it sneered.

Ellie turned, her breath catching in her throat. From the shadows emerged the Frost Reaver, a towering figure of jagged ice and swirling snow. Its eyes glowed with a malevolent blue light, and its form seemed to shift and crackle, as if barely contained by its icy shell.

"Do you really think you can stop me, child?" the Reaver hissed, its voice like the sound of glaciers grinding together. "I am winter's fury, born of despair and doubt. Your little town already belongs to me."

Ellie swallowed hard, clutching the Heart of Winter close to her chest. "You're wrong. Snowhaven hasn't given up hope."

The Frost Reaver laughed, a hollow, echoing sound. "Haven't they? I've seen their hearts. I've felt their despair. They don't believe in magic anymore. They don't believe in you."

The words struck Ellie like a blow. Doubts swirled in her mind—was the Reaver right? The people of Snowhaven had dismissed her warnings, laughed off her stories. Did they truly believe she could save them?

"Ellie, don't listen to it!" Frostwick shouted, darting in front of her. "It's trying to get inside your head!"

The Reaver's glowing eyes narrowed. "And why shouldn't she listen? I'm only speaking the truth." The creature leaned closer, its icy form radiating an oppressive cold. "You're just a little girl playing at being a hero. What makes you think you're special enough to stop me?"

Ellie's hands trembled, the weight of her insecurities threatening to crush her resolve. But then, faintly, she heard the whispers of the winter spirits again.

"Believe in yourself... listen to the light... hope is stronger than fear..."

The words steadied her. She closed her eyes, focusing on the whispers, letting them drown out the Reaver's taunts. Slowly, she felt a warmth building inside her—a spark of determination that grew brighter with every breath.

"You're wrong," Ellie said firmly, opening her eyes to meet the Frost Reaver's gaze. "Snowhaven hasn't lost hope. And neither have I."

The Reaver roared, the sound shaking the chamber. "Then let's see how strong your hope truly is!"

A Battle of Wills

The Frost Reaver lunged, its icy claws slashing toward Ellie. She dodged, clutching the Heart of Winter as its glow intensified. The whispers around her grew louder, clearer, filling the chamber with a harmonious hum that seemed to push back against the Reaver's cold.

"Frostwick, I need your help!" Ellie called.

The snow sprite zipped around the Reaver, creating a flurry of snowflakes that momentarily blinded the creature. "Keep the Heart safe!" Frostwick shouted. "I'll distract it!"

Ellie took a deep breath, holding the Heart of Winter tightly. She could feel its energy coursing through her, a power unlike anything she had ever known. The whispers guided her, urging her to focus, to channel the light within the artifact.

The Reaver lashed out again, its form shifting and cracking as it grew larger, more monstrous. "You cannot stop me!" it bellowed. "Your light is no match for my darkness!"

But Ellie had learned to trust the whispers. She closed her eyes, blocking out the Reaver's roar, and let the spirits' voices guide her.

"Amplify the light... let it shine... hope will prevail..."

Drawing on the whispers, Ellie held the Heart aloft. Its glow intensified, spreading through the chamber in a wave of silvery-blue light. The Reaver screamed as the light touched it, its icy form cracking and splintering.

"No!" the creature howled. "This cannot be!"

Activating the Heart of Winter

"Ellie, now's your chance!" Frostwick shouted, his voice urgent. "Use the Heart!"

Ellie hesitated, the weight of the moment pressing down on her. But the whispers surrounded her, reassuring her, filling her with a sense of purpose. She placed the Heart back on its pedestal, and as her hands left its surface, the artifact pulsed with a radiant energy.

"Guide it with your voice," Frostwick said, his usual playfulness replaced with solemnity. "Speak your hope into the Heart. It will do the rest."

Ellie stepped forward, her voice trembling but steady. "I believe in Snowhaven. I believe in its people, in their strength, and in the magic of winter. I believe in hope."

The Heart responded, its light surging outward in a brilliant explosion that filled the chamber and beyond. The Frost Reaver let out one final, piercing shriek as the light engulfed it, its icy form shattering into a thousand harmless shards.

The light continued to spread, flowing through the labyrinth and into the Whispering Woods, restoring warmth and balance to the frozen landscape. The oppressive cold lifted, replaced by a serene stillness.

A Glimmer of Victory

Ellie collapsed to her knees, exhaustion washing over her. Frostwick landed beside her, his frosty form flickering like a candle. "You did it, kid," he said, a proud grin on his face.

Ellie looked at the Heart of Winter, now glowing softly on its pedestal. "Is it over?" she asked.

"For now," Frostwick said. "The Reaver is gone, but the balance is fragile. The Heart will need a guardian to keep its light strong."

Ellie met his gaze, realization dawning. "You mean me."

Frostwick nodded. "You're the one the whispers chose, Ellie. You've proven your courage and your hope. Snowhaven—and winter—need you."

Though the weight of the task was daunting, Ellie felt a quiet strength within her. She had faced the Frost Reaver and won. She had learned to trust the whispers, to believe in herself. And now, she knew she was ready to embrace her new role as the guardian of the Heart of Winter.

As the two stepped out of the labyrinth and back into the forest, Ellie looked toward Snowhaven, her heart filled with hope. The whispers had guided her this far, and she knew they would continue to guide her in the challenges ahead.

Chapter 5: A New Winter's Harmony

The world felt different as Ellie and Frostwick emerged from the Whispering Woods. The oppressive chill that had gripped the forest was gone, replaced by a gentle, almost comforting cold. Snow fell softly, each flake sparkling like a tiny star. The Heart of Winter, now glowing steadily from its resting place deep in the labyrinth, radiated a warmth that seemed to pulse through the land, restoring balance and harmony.

Ellie glanced at Frostwick, who floated beside her, his mischievous grin tempered by an air of solemn pride. "Did we really do it?" she asked, her voice trembling with awe.

"We did," Frostwick replied, his glowing eyes sparkling like icicles catching the morning sun. "The Frost Reaver has been driven back, its power shattered. And the Heart of Winter? It's alive again, thanks to you."

Ellie smiled, but her mind was already turning to Snowhaven. The whispers had guided her through her journey, but now they carried a different tune—one of joy and unity, a song that called her home. Without hesitation, she and Frostwick began the trek back to the town, their footsteps crunching through the fresh snow.

Snowhaven Reborn

When Ellie reached the edge of Snowhaven, she was struck by how much the town had changed. The early frost that had once clung to every surface with an ominous grip now glittered with a gentle sheen, reflecting the sunlight like a thousand tiny mirrors. The air was crisp but no longer bitter, carrying a freshness that seemed to breathe new life into the town.

As Ellie entered the square, she noticed something remarkable. The townspeople—who had once dismissed her stories and whispers—were gathered outside, their faces turned upward to the falling snow. Laughter echoed through the streets, and children danced in the frost, their cheeks pink with delight. It was as if the weight of the Frost Reaver's despair had been lifted, replaced by a newfound joy.

"Ellie!" a voice called. She turned to see her grandfather, his face alight with pride and relief. He rushed to her, enveloping her in a warm hug. "You did it. I don't know how, but I can feel it. The balance—it's been restored."

Ellie looked into his kind eyes, the emotion of the moment catching her off guard. "I couldn't have done it without the whispers. Or without you."

Her grandfather smiled knowingly. "The whispers may have guided you, but it was your courage and belief that brought us back from the brink. Snowhaven owes you more than it could ever repay."

The Whispers' New Song

As Ellie moved through the square, more townspeople approached her, their skepticism replaced with gratitude. "We didn't believe you before," one woman said, her voice heavy with regret. "But we should have. Thank you, Ellie. You saved us."

Ellie nodded, her cheeks flushing. "It wasn't just me. The winter spirits—those whispers—they believed in all of us. They gave me the strength to keep going."

The wind stirred, carrying a soft melody that seemed to weave through the streets. Ellie paused, tilting her head to listen. The whispers were no longer warnings or cries for help. Instead, they carried messages of joy, hope, and unity—a celebration of the balance that had been restored.

Frostwick fluttered beside her, his grin returning. "You've given them back their voice, Ellie. Winter isn't just a season of cold anymore. It's a season of harmony, thanks to you."

The Guardian of Winter

In the days that followed, Snowhaven embraced its connection to winter's magic. The townspeople began to see the season not as a harsh, unyielding force but as a time of beauty, renewal, and connection. They decorated their homes with frost-kissed wreaths and twinkling lights, and the square was transformed into a wonderland of snow sculptures and icy lanterns.

Ellie, now affectionately known as "Snowhaven's Guardian," became a beacon of hope for the town. She worked with her grandfather to share the stories of the Frost Reaver and the Heart of Winter, teaching the townspeople how to listen to the whispers on the wind and find magic in the everyday.

Frostwick, ever the playful sprite, became a regular sight in the square, delighting children with his frosty tricks and stories of Ellie's bravery. "Stick with me, folks," he'd say, puffing out his chest. "I was there for every step of the adventure."

Whispers of New Adventures

On the first clear night after the Heart of Winter had been restored, Ellie stood outside her house, gazing at the stars. The air was still, the kind of stillness that carried promise. She closed her eyes, letting the wind play with her hair, and listened.

The whispers were soft, almost like a lullaby, but within their melody, Ellie caught something new. Hints of distant lands, of ancient mysteries yet to be uncovered, of adventures waiting just beyond the horizon. The winter spirits were speaking to her again, their voices filled with curiosity and invitation.

"What do you hear?" Frostwick asked, appearing beside her with a curious tilt of his head.

Ellie opened her eyes, a smile playing on her lips. "Whispers of something new. Another journey, maybe."

Frostwick chuckled. "Well, if it's anything like this one, count me in. I'm not done saving the world yet."

Ellie laughed, the sound carrying on the wind. She knew her story with the Heart of Winter wasn't the end—it was the beginning. As long as the whispers called, she would follow, ready to face whatever lay ahead.

The wind picked up, carrying a flurry of snowflakes and the promise of new adventures. And for the first time in a long while, Ellie felt completely at peace, knowing she was exactly where she was meant to be: a guardian of winter, a keeper of harmony, and a listener to the murmurs of magic.

Appendix A: The Legends of Winter Magic

Winter has long been a season cloaked in mystery, its icy breath weaving tales of magic, wonder, and power. From the frosty whispers that echo on the wind to the ethereal glow of the Heart of Winter, these elements of lore have fascinated and inspired generations. Here, we delve into the rich mythology surrounding winter's magic, uncovering the origins and significance of its most enigmatic elements: the frosty whispers, the Heart of Winter, and the Frost Reaver.

The Frosty Whispers

The frosty whispers are the ethereal voices carried by the winter wind, believed to originate from the winter spirits, ancient guardians of the season. These spirits, unseen but ever-present, weave their messages into the cold breeze, whispering secrets, warnings, and blessings to those attuned to their magic.

Origins of the Whispers

According to legend, the whispers began when the first snowfall blanketed the world, marking the birth of winter as a distinct season. The spirits of winter, tasked with maintaining its delicate balance, created the whispers as a way to communicate with mortals. These messages were often cryptic, requiring a deep connection to nature and a pure heart to understand.

Symbolism

- **Guidance:** The whispers often guide those in need, leading them to safety or revealing hidden truths.
- **Warnings:** When the balance of winter is threatened, the whispers grow louder and more urgent, carrying warnings of impending danger.
- **Hope:** In times of despair, the whispers bring comfort, reminding mortals of the beauty and renewal that winter represents.

Connection to the Heart of Winter

The whispers are most potent near the Heart of Winter, the artifact that anchors the season's magic. When the Heart is in harmony, the whispers carry messages of joy and unity. When disrupted, they become fragmented and filled with fear, reflecting the imbalance.

The Heart of Winter

The Heart of Winter is a crystalline artifact that embodies the essence of the season. Its glow symbolizes the balance of winter's dual nature—harsh and unforgiving yet serene and nurturing.

Creation Myth

The Heart of Winter is said to have been forged by the winter spirits themselves, using the first snowfall, the coldest wind, and the light of the northern stars. It was placed in the Frozen Labyrinth to protect it from those who might misuse its power.

The artifact radiates a magic that keeps winter's forces in equilibrium, ensuring that its cold never becomes destructive and its beauty never fades.

Appearance

- **Form:** The Heart appears as a perfectly spherical orb of ice, shot through with veins of glowing blue light.
- **Aura:** It emits a steady, pulsing glow, and those near it often feel a calming warmth, despite its icy nature.
- **Symbolism:** The orb represents unity, resilience, and the cyclical nature of the seasons.

Legends of the Heart

1. **The Protector's Journey:** It is said that only those with a pure heart and a deep respect for nature can activate the Heart's full power.
2. **The Light of Renewal:** When the Heart is restored, it sends a wave of energy through the land, renewing not only winter but the spirits of those who inhabit it.

The Frost Reaver

The Frost Reaver is the antithesis of winter's harmony, a malevolent spirit born from the darkest corners of the season. While winter spirits embody the balance of cold and beauty, the Frost Reaver represents chaos, despair, and endless frost.

Origins of the Frost Reaver

Legends tell of a time when winter grew too powerful, spreading unchecked across the land. From this imbalance, the Frost Reaver was born, feeding on fear and despair. It thrives in darkness and preys on those who lose hope, growing stronger as belief in magic wanes.

Appearance

- **Form:** The Frost Reaver appears as a towering figure of jagged ice and swirling snow, constantly shifting and crackling.
- **Eyes:** Its glowing blue eyes pierce through the cold, filled with malice and hunger.
- **Presence:** The air grows oppressively cold in its presence, and the sound of glaciers grinding fills the silence.

Powers and Weaknesses

- **Powers:**
  - **Despair Manipulation:** The Reaver can amplify fears and doubts, weakening its opponents.
  - **Ice Constructs:** It creates shards and creatures of ice to do its bidding.
  - **Endless Winter:** It spreads a deadly frost that can freeze entire landscapes.
- **Weaknesses:**
  - **The Heart of Winter:** The artifact's light can weaken and banish the Reaver.
  - **Hope:** The Frost Reaver is vulnerable to hope, courage, and belief in magic, which counteract its influence.

Key Locations of Winter Magic
1. The Whispering Woods

- **Description:** A dense, snow-covered forest at the edge of Snowhaven, filled with towering evergreens and shimmering frost. The woods are alive with whispers and a faint blue light that guides travelers.
- **Legend:** The forest is said to be the gateway to the Frozen Labyrinth and a haven for winter spirits.

2. The Frozen Labyrinth

- **Description:** A sprawling maze of towering ice walls, shimmering with shifting reflections and illusions. The labyrinth is alive, filled with puzzles, traps, and challenges designed to test the worthiness of those who enter.
- **Legend:** It was created by the winter spirits to protect the Heart of Winter, ensuring only the purest souls could reach it.

3. The Heart of Winter

- **Description:** The focal point of winter's magic, located at the heart of the labyrinth. Its glow illuminates the icy chamber where it rests, surrounded by an aura of peace and power.
- **Legend:** The artifact is the key to restoring balance to winter and banishing the Frost Reaver.

Conclusion

The legends of winter magic remind us that even in the coldest, darkest times, there is beauty, balance, and hope. The frosty whispers, the Heart of Winter, and the Frost Reaver are not just elements of mythology but reflections of the eternal struggle between light and shadow, despair and hope. As guardians of winter, we are called to listen, to believe, and to protect the harmony that makes this season magical.

Appendix B: The Creatures of Frosty Whispers

Winter's magic is alive, woven into the fabric of the season by a host of fantastical beings. These creatures, both benevolent and malevolent, play crucial roles in shaping the frosty whispers and maintaining—or disrupting—the delicate balance of winter. Below is an in-depth guide to the magical beings featured in the story, including their origins, abilities, and fascinating traits.

1. Frostwick: The Snow Sprite Extraordinaire
Origins

Frostwick belongs to a race of mischievous yet kind-hearted beings known as snow sprites. These tiny creatures are said to have been born from the first playful snowfall, imbued with the joy and wonder that winter brings. Each snow sprite has a unique personality, and Frostwick is no exception—a charming mix of cleverness, mischief, and loyalty.

Appearance

- **Size:** No taller than a child's boot, Frostwick is diminutive yet dazzling.
- **Form:** A figure made entirely of compact snow, with crystalline frost forming intricate patterns across his body.
- **Eyes:** Glowing icy-blue orbs filled with curiosity and warmth.
- **Aura:** Frostwick radiates a chill, but it's a playful, invigorating cold rather than a harsh freeze.

Abilities

1. **Frost Manipulation:** Frostwick can shape snow and ice, creating delicate frost patterns or playful snowflakes.
2. **Illusion Crafting:** He uses his magic to cast harmless illusions, often for entertainment or distraction.

3. **Whisper Amplification:** As a conduit for the frosty whispers, Frostwick can amplify their guidance to help those in need.
4. **Rapid Movement:** His small size and light form allow him to zip through the air with surprising speed.

Role in Winter's Balance

Frostwick acts as a guide and protector, particularly for mortals who are chosen by the whispers. He ensures that the Heart of Winter remains secure, offering his unique blend of cunning and courage to aid in its defense.

Fun Facts

- **Favorite Pastime:** Frostwick loves sculpting tiny snow castles and challenging other sprites to races through snowdrifts.
- **Favorite Treat:** He's particularly fond of icicle pops, a delicacy made from enchanted snow.
- **Quirks:** Frostwick hums softly when concentrating on his illusions and often leaves a trail of glittering frost wherever he goes.

Tips for Interacting with Snow Sprites

- **Be Playful:** Snow sprites are naturally mischievous and respond well to lightheartedness.
- **Respect Their Space:** Though friendly, sprites value their autonomy. Avoid trying to capture or confine them.
- **Offer Snow Gifts:** Presenting a beautifully shaped snowball or frost flower is a sign of goodwill.

2. The Frost Reaver: Winter's Shadow
Origins

The Frost Reaver is a malevolent spirit born from winter's imbalance. When the season grows too harsh or when despair takes root in human hearts, the Reaver emerges, feeding on fear, doubt, and hopelessness. It is a manifestation of winter's darker side, a reminder of the season's potential for destruction when harmony is lost.

Appearance

- **Size:** Towering and imposing, the Frost Reaver stands as tall as the tallest pines.
- **Form:** A jagged, ever-shifting mass of ice and snow, its edges sharp and menacing.
- **Eyes:** Piercing, glowing blue orbs that radiate malice.
- **Aura:** The Frost Reaver exudes an oppressive cold that freezes everything in its vicinity.

Abilities

1. **Despair Amplification:** The Frost Reaver can instill fear and doubt, sapping the hope of those who encounter it.
2. **Ice Constructs:** It creates icy minions and barriers to aid in its destructive goals.
3. **Endless Frost:** The Reaver spreads a deadly cold that can freeze entire landscapes in moments.
4. **Shape-Shifting:** Its form is not fixed, allowing it to adapt its icy body to intimidate or attack.

Role in Winter's Balance

The Frost Reaver seeks to disrupt the balance of winter, plunging the world into eternal cold. Its presence signals a grave imbalance in the season's magic, requiring the intervention of a strong-hearted guardian.

Fun Facts

- **Weakness:** The Frost Reaver cannot withstand pure light, hope, or the energy of the Heart of Winter.
- **Tales of Terror:** Some legends claim the Frost Reaver was once a winter spirit that fell to corruption, though this remains unconfirmed.
- **Unseen Form:** When dormant, the Reaver exists as a faint shadow in the frost, waiting for despair to call it forth.

Tips for Facing the Frost Reaver

- **Stay Hopeful:** The Reaver thrives on despair; hope and courage weaken its power.
- **Use Light:** Bright, focused light can momentarily stun or drive back the creature.
- **Avoid Direct Combat:** The Frost Reaver is nearly indestructible by physical means; rely on winter magic and the Heart of Winter.

3. The Winter Spirits
Origins

The winter spirits are ancient, elemental beings that personify the essence of the season. Invisible to most, they communicate through frosty whispers, guiding mortals and maintaining the balance of winter's forces.

Appearance

- **Form:** When visible, they appear as ephemeral figures made of swirling snow and frost, their edges shimmering like ice crystals in sunlight.
- **Aura:** They exude a calming presence, their movements fluid and graceful.

Abilities

1. **Frosty Whispers:** The spirits send messages through the wind, offering guidance, warnings, or blessings.
2. **Balance Keepers:** They subtly manipulate winter's forces to ensure harmony between cold and warmth.
3. **Blessings:** Winter spirits can imbue mortals with temporary abilities, such as enhanced endurance in the cold or an intuitive sense of direction.

Role in Winter's Balance

As guardians of the season, winter spirits are the unseen custodians of its magic. They watch over the Heart of Winter, ensuring it remains protected and balanced.

Fun Facts

- **Lifespan:** Winter spirits are eternal, fading only when winter itself disappears.
- **Music of the Wind:** Their whispers often carry melodies, which some believe are fragments of ancient songs.
- **Favored Humans:** They are drawn to those who show kindness and respect for nature.

Other Frosty Creatures
1. Ice Owls

- **Appearance:** Large, white-feathered owls with eyes that shimmer like frost.
- **Abilities:** They serve as messengers for the winter spirits, their calls echoing through the woods.
- **Fun Fact:** Ice owls can spot warmth, making them excellent guides in frozen landscapes.

2. Frost Foxes

- **Appearance:** Small, sleek foxes with fur that glows faintly in moonlight.
- **Abilities:** Known for their speed and agility, frost foxes are protectors of the Whispering Woods.
- **Fun Fact:** They leave trails of sparkling frost wherever they run, marking safe paths through the snow.

Conclusion

The creatures of frosty whispers are as diverse as winter itself—playful, dangerous, mysterious, and awe-inspiring. Together, they weave the magic that makes the season not just a time of cold but a time of wonder, reminding us that even in the harshest storms, there is beauty, balance, and light.

<u>Message from the Author:</u>

I hope you enjoyed this book, I love astrology and knew there was not a book such as this out on the shelf. I love metaphysical items as well. Please check out my other books:

-Life of Government Benefits

-My life of Hell

-My life with Hydrocephalus

-Red Sky

-World Domination:Woman's rule

-World Domination:Woman's Rule 2: The War

-Life and Banishment of Apophis: book 1

-The Kidney Friendly Diet

-The Ultimate Hemp Cookbook

-Creating a Dispensary(legally)

-Cleanliness throughout life: the importance of showering from childhood to adulthood.

-Strong Roots: The Risks of Overcoddling children

-Hemp Horoscopes: Cosmic Insights and Earthly Healing

- Celestial Hemp Navigating the Zodiac: Through the Green Cosmos

-Astrological Hemp: Aligning The Stars with Earth's Ancient Herb

-The Astrological Guide to Hemp: Stars, Signs, and Sacred Leaves

-Green Growth: Innovative Marketing Strategies for your Hemp Products and Dispensary

-Cosmic Cannabis

-Astrological Munchies

-Henry The Hemp

-Zodiacal Roots: The Astrological Soul Of Hemp

- **Green Constellations: Intersection of Hemp and Zodiac**

-Hemp in The Houses: An astrological Adventure Through The Cannabis Galaxy

-Galactic Ganja Guide

Heavenly Hemp

Zodiac Leaves

Doctor Who Astrology

Cannastrology

Stellar Satvias and Cosmic Indicas

<u>Celestial Cannabis: A Zodiac Journey</u>

AstroHerbology: The Sky and The Soil: Volume 1

AstroHerbology:Celestial Cannabis:Volume 2

Cosmic Cannabis Cultivation

The Starry Guide to Herbal Harmony: Volume 1

The Starry Guide to Herbal Harmony: Cannabis Universe: Volume 2

Yugioh Astrology: Astrological Guide to Deck, Duels and more

Nightmare Mansion: Echoes of The Abyss

Nightmare Mansion 2: Legacy of Shadows

Nightmare Mansion 3: Shadows of the Forgotten

Nightmare Mansion 4: Echoes of the Damned

The Life and Banishment of Apophis: Book 2

Nightmare Mansion: Halls of Despair

<u>Healing with Herb: Cannabis and Hydrocephalus</u>

<u>Planetary Pot: Aligning with Astrological Herbs: Volume 1</u>

Fast Track to Freedom: 30 Days to Financial Independence Using AI, Assets, and Agile Hustles

<u>Cosmic Hemp Pathways</u>

How to Become Financially Free in 30 Days: 10,000 Paths to Prosperity

Zodiacal Herbage: Astrological Insights: Volume 1

Nightmare Mansion: Whispers in the Walls

The Daleks Invade Atlantis

Henry the hemp and Hydrocephalus

10X The Kidney Friendly Diet

Cannabis Universe: Adult coloring book

Hemp Astrology: The Healing Power of the Stars

Zodiacal Herbage: Astrological Insights: Cannabis Universe: Volume 2

<u>Planetary Pot: Aligning with Astrological Herbs: Cannabis Universes: Volume 2</u>

Doctor Who Meets the Replicators and SG-1: The Ultimate Battle for Survival

Nightmare Mansion: Curse of the Blood Moon

<u>The Celestial Stoner: A Guide to the Zodiac</u>

Cosmic Pleasures: Sex Toy Astrology for Every Sign

Hydrocephalus Astrology: Navigating the Stars and Healing Waters

Lapis and the Mischievous Chocolate Bar

Celestial Positions: Sexual Astrology for Every Sign

Apophis's Shadow Work Journal: : A Journey of Self-Discovery and Healing

Kinky Cosmos: Sexual Kink Astrology for Every Sign

Digital Cosmos: The Astrological Digimon Compendium

Stellar Seeds: The Cosmic Guide to Growing with Astrology

Apophis's Daily Gratitude Journal

Cat Astrology: Feline Mysteries of the Cosmos

The Cosmic Kama Sutra: An Astrological Guide to Sexual Positions

Unleash Your Potential: A Guided Journal Powered by AI Insights

Whispers of the Enchanted Grove

Cosmic Pleasures: An Astrological Guide to Sexual Kinks

369, 12 Manifestation Journal

Whisper of the nocturne journal(blank journal for writing or drawing)

Whispers of the Harvest: The Corn Mother's Journal

The Evergreen Spellbook

The Doctor Meets the Boogeyman

The White Witch of Rose Hall's SpellBook

The Gingerbread Golem's Shadow: A Study in Sweet Darkness

The Gingerbread Golem Codex: An Academic Exploration of Sweet Myths

The Gingerbread Golem Grimoire: Sweet Magicks and Spells for the Festive Witch

The Curse of the Gingerbread Golem

10-minute Christmas Crafts for kids

<u>Christmas Crisis Solutions: The Ultimate Last-Minute Survival Guide</u>

Gingerbread Golem Recipes: Holiday Treats with a Magical Twist

The Infinite Key: Unlocking Mystical Secrets of the Ages

Enchanted Yule: A Wiccan and Pagan Guide to a Magical and Memorable Season

Dinosaurs of Power: Unlocking Ancient Magick

Astro-Dinos: The Cosmic Guide to Prehistoric Wisdom

Gallifrey's Yule Logs: A Festive Doctor Who Cookbook

The Dino Grimoire: Secrets of Prehistoric Magick

The Gift They Never Knew They Needed

The Gingerbread Golem's Culinary Alchemy: Enchanting Recipes for a Sweetly Dark Feast

A Time Lord Christmas: Holiday Adventures with the Doctor

Krampusproofing Your Home: Defensive Strategies for Yule

Silent Frights: A Collection of Christmas Creepypastas to Chill Your Bones

Santa Raptor's Jolly Carnage: A Dino-Claus Christmas Tale

Prehistoric Palettes: A Dino Wicca Coloring Journey

The Christmas Wishkeeper Chronicles

The Starlight Sleigh: A Holiday Journey

Elf Secrets: The True Magic of the North Pole

Candy Cane Conjurations
Cooking with Kids: Recipes Under 20 Minutes
Doctor Who: The TARDIS Confiscation
The Anxiety First Aid Kit: Quick Tools to Calm Your Mind
If you want solar for your home go here: https://www.harborso-lar.live/apophisenterprises/

Get Some Tarot cards: https://www.makeplayingcards.com/sell/apophis-occult-shop

Get some shirts: https://www.bonfire.com/store/apophis-shirt-emporium/

<u>**Instagrams:**</u>
@apophis_enterprises,
@apophisbookemporium,
@apophisscardshop
Twitter: @apophisenterpr1
Tiktok:@apophisenterprise
Youtube: @sg1fan23477, @FiresideRetreatKingdom
Hive: @sg1fan23477
CheeLee: @SG1fan23477

Podcast: Apophis Chat Zone: https://open.spotify.com/show/
5zXbrCLEV2xzCp8ybrfHsk?si=fb4d4fdbdce44dec

Newsletter: https://apophiss-newsletter-27c897.beehiiv.com/

If you want to support me or see posts of other projects that I have come over to: **buymeacoffee.com/mpetchinskg**
I post there daily several times a day

Get your Dinowicca or Christmas themed digital products, especially Santa Raptor songs and other musics. Here: **https://sg1fan23477.gumroad.com**

Apophis Yuletide Digital has not only digital Christmas items, but it will have all things with Dinowicca as well as other Digital products.

www.ingramcontent.com/pod-product-compliance
Lightning Source LLC
Chambersburg PA
CBHW061315140726
47998CB00006B/2406